ACTIVE
CITIZENSHIP
TODAY

Learning about Other People and Cultures

Jan Mader

Cavendish
Square

New York

Published in 2018 by Cavendish Square Publishing, LLC
243 5th Avenue, Suite 136, New York, NY 10016

Copyright © 2018 by Cavendish Square Publishing, LLC

First Edition

Library of Congress Cataloging-in-Publication Data

Names: Mader, Jan (Janet G), author.
Title: Learning about other people and cultures / Jan Mader.
Description: New York : Cavendish Square Publishing, [2018] |
Series: Active citizenship today | Includes index.
Identifiers: LCCN 2017020196 (print) | LCCN 2017034289 (ebook) | ISBN 9781502629272 (E-book) |
ISBN 9781502629241 (pbk.) | ISBN 9781502629265 (library bound) | ISBN 9781502629258 (6 pack)
Subjects: LCSH: Immigrants--United States--Juvenile literature. | Cultural pluralism--United States--Juvenile literature. | Multiculturalism--United States--Juvenile literature.
Classification: LCC E184.A1 (ebook) | LCC E184.A1 M24 2018 (print) | DDC 305.8--dc23
LC record available at https://lccn.loc.gov/2017020196

Editorial Director: David McNamara
Editor: Fletcher Doyle
Copy Editor: Nathan Heidelberger
Associate Art Director: Amy Greenan
Designer: Joe Parenteau
Production Coordinator: Karol Szymczuk
Photo Research: J8 Media

Printed in the United States of America

CONTENTS

1 Look Around You 5

2 Welcome 13

3 Show You Care............................ 21

Glossary 27

Find Out More.............................. 29

Index...................................... 31

About the Author.......................... 32

1

Look Around You

Look around your class. Does everyone look the same as you? Does everyone sound the same as you? Probably not. Maybe a new boy sounds different when he talks. Perhaps he came from another state. He speaks English, but it sounds different from the way you talk. People from other states might have a different **accent**.

Opposite: Friends come in all shapes, sizes, and colors!

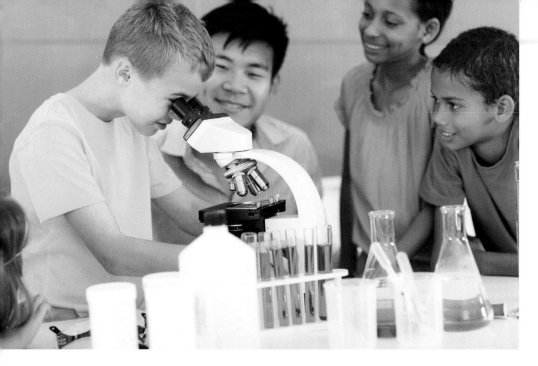

Teamwork can help everyone learn better.

Maybe two kids wear glasses. They don't see as well as you. When they wear glasses, they can see fine! Kids learn differently. Some kids

Some kids need glasses to see in class.

Learning about Other People and Cultures

read quickly. Other kids are better at math. Some kids leave the room with a different teacher. This teacher helps kids learn in their own way.

Bullies

On the playground, kids play games. Many like soccer. Girls like soccer as much as the boys. Sometimes boys don't want the girls to play. They

Bullies hurt people inside and out.

Girls should not be left out of games.

think the girls aren't good enough. Is this fair? It is not. Sometimes **bullies** try to stop girls from playing. They tell them they are not good enough. They tell them they are not fast enough.

BAD WAY TO BE

Most bullies don't understand what they do is very bad. They don't know how it feels to be bullied. Bullies have not learned kindness and respect.

Bullies make fun of kids with **disabilities**, too. Kids with disabilities might be in a wheelchair. They might not be able to walk like your other friends. It is mean to make fun of other people. What can you do? Tell an adult what is happening. Take time to talk to your friend with a disability.

Kids with disabilities might feel alone on a playground.

At Home

Everyone has a family. Not all families are the same. Pretend you live in a home with just your mother. Your friend across the street has two parents. You can see him throw the ball with his dad. Would that make you feel badly? If it does, ask your mom to throw the ball to you. Remember, moms can throw balls just like dads. Perhaps your friend smells fresh cookies. The smell comes from your house. Ask your friend over for cookies!

Moms can be really good at flipping a Frisbee.

Some families have two moms. Others have two dads. Maybe your neighbor is Mexican. He is your age. Could you invite him for cookies, too? Maybe he would invite you and your mom for dinner one night. You could eat something new.

When you go to your Mexican friend's house, you might see his grandma. You might be surprised to find out that his grandma lives there. You might think how awesome it would be if your grandma or grandpa could live with you. Your friend might think how awesome it would be to have a quiet house. Getting to know other people is fun.

Grandma's food is really delicious.
You can eat something new at a friend's house.

2

Welcome

Imagine moving to a new town. You might live in a neighborhood. You might live on a farm. Everything would be new to you. Moving is never easy. It's even worse if you move away from all your friends. You might feel angry or sad.

What might make you feel better?

Opposite: Say hello to a kid moving in. New kids left their friends behind.

WISE SAGE STUDENT

There are two thousand kids in San Diego's Student Safety Patrol. Only one gets to be colonel. In 2016, Shelby Sparks got the honor. The Sage Canyon student was chosen because she was dedicated. She showed respect for everyone. She was reliable and trustworthy. Shelby was a good citizen.

If you saw a child your age riding a bike, would you feel better? What if the child stopped to say hello? Would you feel better then? You might! When you make a new friend, it is like planting a garden. Sometimes a seed grows and grows. Other times it just grows a little. It's OK either way. You can decide how fast you want your friendship to grow!

Waving hello can make a new kid feel welcome.

Respect

Respect is the key to everything. We all have feelings. We all want to know someone cares for us. We all want to be treated well. What would happen if a **blind** child lived nearby? Would you feel afraid of her because she is different? You might at first. Then you would

This blind boy uses a white cane to feel where objects are.

remember your manners. Ask if it is OK to go visit her. Tell her who you are. Ask about her. Find out what she likes to do. Tell her what you like to do. Think about things you could do together.

It would be easy to talk to a blind person. They can hear. What if a new girl moved to your neighborhood? What if she came from Korea? How could you talk to someone who doesn't speak your language? **Language barriers** are hard! What can you

RESPECT CHECKLIST

If you want to show respect, do these things:

✓ Listen well

✓ Be kind

✓ Value differences

✓ Use good manners

✓ Encourage

do? First of all, **include** your friend in games you play. Your Korean friend doesn't need to speak English to help you finish a puzzle.

Words are not needed to start a friendship.

New kids can see your kindness.

While you are putting together a puzzle, your friend will be listening to you. She will learn new words while you talk and share. She will see your kindness.

Let's Talk!

"Please" and "thank you" might be your friend's first American words. Why? You have used good manners. You have **accepted** your friend just the way she is. Soon your new friend will speak English. Then you need to be a good listener. Hear what she has to say. Share ideas with her. Listen to her ideas.

BAD HELP

Lucy Lee moved to the United States from Korea. She was seven years old. Children at school laughed at her way of talking. One day she needed to tell her teacher something. She asked a boy for help. He taught her bad words. Lucy said the bad words to her teacher. Lucy got in trouble. Now Lucy is a teacher. She understands new kids and their problems.

Learning about Other People and Cultures

Lucy Lee understands new students.

Begin to build **trust**. Tell your friend what you think of a book. Ask her what she thinks. You don't have to think the same way. You don't have to like the same things. You do need to be respectful. Remember the seed in the garden? Seeds grow when they are watered and fed. Friendships grow when you listen, talk, and care!

Learn to share ideas with new friends.

3

Show You Care

Doing the right thing is not always easy. Sometimes it is hard. When new children move near you, take the time to greet them. When there is a disabled child in your class, be kind. Others will be watching you. You are the shining example.

Opposite: The lunchroom should be a happy place. It is where everyone sits together.

Offer to sit next to a new child in the lunchroom. Offer to stay with a new child on the playground. Try to show new children the games you play at school. Soon the new children will trust you. They will feel welcome in your school and neighborhood.

Learn More

Learn about other places. Ask your teacher if you can have a Taste New Foods Day. Everyone can bring in a favorite food. What will your Korean

It's fun to try food from other places.

friend bring? Ever heard of kimchi? Your friend from North Carolina may bring in grits or cornbread. It's fun to taste and smell new foods.

Decorate the desks in your room with pictures and maps. Ask your teacher to put a big map of the United States on the wall. Everyone in your class can put a dot on the state where they

Find out where your friends are from.

were born. What about your Korean friend? Do the same thing with a map of the world. Think about how Korea is so far away.

Get to know your Korean friend. You can learn about her Korean **culture**. You can begin to understand about her life in Korea. North Carolina is not as far away as Korea. If you live in Ohio, it's still far! Find out how Southern culture is different from culture in the Midwest.

Take time to listen to learn about others.

Talk and Listen

Take time to talk to children who are different from you. They might want to know about you. Think about how you are different. See how you are the same. Draw a picture of your family to share.

Learning about Other People and Cultures

Tell a story about your family. Ask new children about their families.

WRITE A BOOK

Pretend you are a reporter. Find out about your new friend. Ask about his family. Ask about his customs. Ask what he likes about America. Write a book about your friend. Share the book with your class. See if you can put the book in your library. Start your own library right in your classroom. You can write. You can draw. You can share! Other people will want to learn what you know.

Go to the school library. Get a book about Mexico. Look at the pictures. Ask your Mexican friend about his culture. Really listen while he shares his story.

Learn about cultures in the school library.

Get permission to start a school newspaper. Maybe you could start a blog on the school website. Become a reporter. **Interview** new students once a month. Get a photo of the new children to put in the newspaper or on the blog. Celebrate differences!

Differences are things to celebrate.

Learning about Other People and Cultures

Glossary

accent A way of pronouncing words that is common among people in a region.

accepted To think of someone as belonging to a group.

blind Unable to see because of an injury or a condition.

bullies People who frighten, hurt, or threaten other people.

culture The values, beliefs, and behaviors of a group of people.

disability A condition that limits a person's physical or mental abilities.

include To let someone or something be part of a group or an activity.

interview To ask someone questions to get information.

language barrier The difficulty of talking to someone who only speaks a different language.

respect Thinking good things about who a person is and about the way he or she acts.

trust Belief that someone is reliable and honest.

Find Out More

Books

Behrens, Janice. *We Are Alike, We Are Different*. We the Kids. New York: Scholastic Books for Young Readers, 2009.

Martineau, Susan. *Dealing with Differences*. Positive Steps. Mankato, MN: Smart Apple Media, 2012.

Websites

Daniel Tiger PBS

http://pbskids.org/daniel

This PBS website allows kids to learn about differences while they play with Daniel Tiger and his friends.

Kids' Quest: Autism

https://www.cdc.gov/ncbddd/kids/autism.html

This website from the Centers for Disease Control and Prevention helps children learn about disabilities.

Talking with Trees

http://talkingtreebooks.com/definition/what-is-respect.html

This website from a children's book publisher is about respect. It's about how you feel about someone and how you treat them.

Index

Page numbers in **boldface** are illustrations.

accent, 5
accepted, 18
blind, 15–16, **15**
bullies, **7**, 8–9
culture, 24–25
disability, 9, **9**, 15–16, **15**, 21
family, 9–11, **10**, **11**, 24–25
food, 10–11, **11**, 22–23, **22**
include, 17
interview, 26

kindness, 8, 16–17, 21
Korea, 16–18, 22–24
language barrier, 16–17
learning English, 17–18, 23
Lee, Lucy, 18, **19**
library, 25, **26**
listening, 16–19, 25
moving, **12**, 13–14, 16, 18
new kids, 5, **12**, 13–14, 16–19, 21–22, 25–26
respect, 8, 10, 14–16, 19
Sparks, Shelby, 14
trust, 19, 22
writing, 25

About the Author

Jan Mader has written many books for children. Her books can be found in classrooms and libraries around the world. Jan almost always has some sort of animal in her stories. Her favorite animal to write about is her horse, Tango! In the winter, she loves to go sledding with Tango. Jan and her husband live in Columbus, Ohio, with their dogs Sammy, Charlie, and Annabelle.

Learning about Other People and Cultures